D0562262

SPORK OUT
OF ORBIT

For Sue Kassirer—N.W.

To Ken, who always helps to make this strange Earth life a fun adventure—J.W.

Text copyright © 2016 by Nan Walker
Illustrations copyright © 2016 by Jessica Warrick
Galaxy Scout Activities illustrations copyright © 2016 by Kane Press, Inc.
Galaxy Scout Activities illustrations by Nadia DiMattia

Library of Congress Cataloging-in-Publication Data

Walker, Nan.
Spork out of orbit / by Nan Walker ; illustrated by Jessica Warrick.
pages   cm. — (How to be an earthling ; 1)
Summary: To earn his Solo Explorer badge, Spork the alien lands on Earth to study the customs of Mrs. Buckle's third grade class.
ISBN 978-1-57565-819-3 (pbk) — ISBN 978-1-57565-818-6 (reinforced library binding) — ISBN 978-1-57565-820-9 (ebook)
[1. Extraterrestrial beings—Fiction. 2. Schools—Fiction. 3. Humorous stories.]
I. Warrick, Jessica, illustrator. II. Title.
PZ7.W153643Sp 2016
[Fic]—dc23
2015010627

1 3 5 7 9 10 8 6 4 2

First published in the United States of America in 2016 by Kane Press, Inc.
Printed in the United States of America

Book Design: Edward Miller

How to Be an Earthling is a trademark of Kane Press, Inc.

Visit us online at **www.kanepress.com**

Like us on Facebook
facebook.com/kanepress

Follow us on Twitter
@KanePress

CONTENTS

SPORK OUT OF ORBIT

by Nan Walker
illustrated by Jessica Warrick

The KANE PRESS
New York

Spork

Trixie Lopez

Mrs. Buckle

Jack Donnelly

Grace Hanford

Jo Jo

Newton Miller

BEEP.
BEEEEEP.
Is this thing on? Oh. Okay.

Hey, you guys! I'm here! I am about to land! I've reached my planet, and I found a training center. I am going to learn EVERYTHING about the way they do things here. Yes, sir, that Solo Explorer badge is MINE.

I know you're thinking of the time we all went camping in that spiral galaxy. Honestly, I still have no idea how my pod got loose and drifted into space! And, sure, there was that other time I blew up the troop leader's . . . Never mind. Accidents happen, right?

The point is, this time is different. This time is going to be perfect.

I'm right over the training center now. I've got my landing all set up. I'm going to touch down as lightly as a—

CRASH!

Oops.

1

GREETINGS, EARTHLINGS!

Trixie drummed her feet. She tapped her fingers on her desk. She glanced out the window at the playground. Then she looked at her word puzzle and sighed.

Word puzzles on Wednesdays. Math games on Mondays. Spelling bees on Fridays.

If only something *different* would happen!

Trixie liked her teacher, Mrs. Buckle. She liked her best friends, Newton and Grace, and the rest of her classmates. Well . . . she couldn't exactly say she *liked* Jack. But she didn't mind him. Much.

All in all, third grade was pretty nice. Still . . .

With another sigh, Trixie looked out the window again.

CRASH! CRASH!

Something big and shiny hit the jungle gym. It skidded across the monkey bars, bounced off the slide, and landed on the hopscotch court in a shower of sparks.

CRASH!

It was as big as a car, but flatter and rounder. It was a . . .

"Flying saucer!" Trixie yelled.

"Trixie, please raise your hand instead of—" Mrs. Buckle's eyes went to the window. "Oh, my," she said. "OH, MY."

The classroom had a door that opened to the playground. Everyone ran out the door.

Trixie reached the flying saucer first. But before she could touch it, Newton grabbed her arm. "It might be dangerous!" he said.

"That's not a real spaceship," Jack scoffed. "I bet it blew out of somebody's yard."

He kicked it. The bubble-shaped

top flipped open, and an orange alien popped out. "Greetings, Earthlings!" he said in a squeaky voice.

"Aaaahhh!" Jack yelled, jumping back.

"Aaaahhh!" the alien squeaked, and fell off the flying saucer.

He lay on his back, arms and legs
wiggling. To Trixie, he looked like a giant
bug.

Grace helped the alien up. "Are you
okay?"

"Happens to me all the time," the
alien said cheerfully. "Now, where was
I? Oh, right. Greetings,
Earthlings! I've
come to your
Earthling
training
center
to learn all
about your
Earthling
customs."

"Earthling training center?" Trixie repeated.

Newton whispered, "I think he means school."

The third graders buzzed with excitement.

"An alien in our class!"

"Even the fifth graders don't have an alien!"

"Please, Mrs. Buckle? Can we keep him? *Pleeeeease*?"

Mrs. Buckle frowned. "I really don't think . . ."

The children groaned.

Trixie bit her lip. She had wished for something different to happen in third grade. An alien landing was about as different as it got. He just had to be allowed to stay!

"He can sit near us," she told Mrs. Buckle. "Right, Newton?"

Newton shot a nervous look at the alien, but nodded.

Mrs. Buckle said, "That's not—"

"And think of all the stuff that we could learn from him!" Trixie went on. "I mean, I've never been to any other planet except Earth. Have you?"

"Well, no, I haven't." The teacher smiled. "All right. I guess we can give it a try." Turning to the alien, she said, "Welcome to our . . . uh, Earthling training center!"

Everybody cheered.

Trixie was glad she had been looking

out the window when the flying saucer landed. But she didn't think she would be looking out the window much anymore.

Not with a space alien in her class!

+ = FUN!

2

COSMIC!

"My name is Beatrix," Trixie told the alien as Mrs. Buckle herded everyone inside. "But everybody calls me Trixie. What's your name?"

The alien smiled. "My name is—" He made a long hissing, spitting, hacking noise.

Trixie tried to repeat it. "*Ssss . . . poh . . .
oh . . . ORK . . .* Spork?"

"What kind of a name is that?" Jack
scoffed. "Sounds like a ferret throwing
up!"

Trixie scowled at Jack.

"Jack, that's not the way we speak
to each other in this classroom," Mrs.
Buckle said. She pointed to the poster

hanging near the chalkboard. "We treat each other with respect, remember?"

The alien scanned the poster eagerly. "Look at all these interesting Earthling customs! 'Keeping our hands to ourselves'? Wait till the other scouts hear *that*!"

RESPECT MEANS... ←

- Following directions
- Raising our hands to speak
- Paying attention to our work
- Keeping our hands to ourselves
- Saying please and thank you
- Taking care of property
- Treating others as we would like to be treated (the Golden Rule)

"Don't you have that rule on your planet, uh . . . Spork?" Mrs. Buckle asked.

"We don't need it." The alien held up his hands. "Our hands don't come off."

The third graders laughed.

"Ours don't come off either," Grace explained. "Keeping your hands to yourself means don't grab or poke."

"Oh," Spork said. Trixie couldn't tell if he was disappointed or relieved.

Mrs. Buckle asked the alien to come to the front of the room to tell the class about himself. Spork explained that he was a Galaxy Scout trying to earn his Solo Explorer badge.

"How many badges do you have so far?" Grace asked.

"Well . . . actually, not so many," Spork admitted. "In fact, none."

"I've already earned two badges, and I've only been a peewee scout since August," Jack bragged.

"Cosmic!" Spork said. "What for? Deep space diving? Rocket races?"

"Decorating a bookmark," Jack mumbled. "And checking my dog for fleas."

Spork told the class about the other planets he had visited with the Galaxy Scouts. "And then there was that time we took a field trip to the moon of Mercury—"

Jack jumped up. "You couldn't have! I watched a TV show about the solar system, and it said Mercury doesn't even *have* a moon."

Spork turned a deeper shade of orange. Trixie thought he was blushing.

"No," he agreed, looking ashamed. "Not anymore."

"Does that mean what I *think* it means?" Newton whispered to Trixie. "Yikes!"

Trixie grinned.

"Well, Spork," Mrs. Buckle said. "Having you here should be quite . . . interesting. And we'll do our very best to teach you our Earthling ways."

The alien beamed. "That's good, because I only have one day to learn all about Earth. Then I have to go back to my troop."

Trixie felt the smile slide right off her face. Only one day?

Spork *couldn't* leave so soon!

3

FLYING SPACE ROCKS

Trixie thought the clock on the wall
of Mrs. Buckle's classroom must be
broken. Usually the minute hand crept
slowly. This morning it seemed to race.
Spork's one day on Earth was going by
too fast!

Third grade was definitely *different* with an alien in the classroom. Spork mistook the class hamster, Jo Jo, for a small, furry third grader. He thought crayons were a chewy treat. And when Mrs. Buckle turned from the board with a piece of chalk in her raised hand, Spork dove under the table.

Trixie leaned down. "What are you doing?"

Cautiously, Spork looked up. "Isn't she going to throw that chalk?"

"Do teachers on your planet throw things at you?" Newton asked the alien.

"Of course!" Spork crawled out. "That's how we learn."

Jack crossed his arms. "How could that possibly help you learn?"

"We learn to duck," Spork said. "It's very useful for avoiding flying space rocks."

Everyone laughed, except for Jack. Even Mrs. Buckle smiled.

"Spork, I try to follow the Golden Rule," she said, pointing to the RESPECT poster. "And I would NOT like to have anyone throw chalk at me!"

It was the weirdest, most exciting school day ever, and Trixie didn't want it to end. She had to think of some way to get Spork to stay!

At morning recess, everybody swarmed around the flying saucer. Spork let the children climb all over it. He even let them take turns sitting in his pilot seat.

When Trixie slid into the seat, her foot kicked something that rolled squishily away. She reached

down and picked up what looked like a
small balloon filled with Jell-O.

"What's this?" she asked, tossing it
down to Spork.

"Whoa!" Spork caught it and set it
gently on the ground
under the flying
saucer.

"Careful with that Gloop! You don't want it to burst."

"Gloop?" Trixie asked.

"Don't you have that here?" Spork said. "Gloop fixes everything. It's great when I—uh, land with a bit of a bump."

Trixie looked over the flying saucer. "Did you break something when you crashed?"

Spork turned a deeper orange again. He glanced around.

"Did everyone see me crash?"

"Just me, I think," she said.

The orange faded slightly. "Oh, well. My ship might not be exactly spaceworthy right now. But with a little Gloop, it will be good as new."

When the bell rang, the children ran to line up by the door. Spork shut the bubble top and dashed after them.

Trixie was about to follow, when she spotted the Gloop lying on the ground.

"Spork!" she called, but he didn't hear her.

She picked up the Gloop and started toward him. Then she stopped.

Spork said he would need the Gloop to fix the flying saucer before he left Earth.

So if he didn't have the Gloop . . . he'd have to stay.

Trixie stuffed the Gloop into her coat pocket and ran to catch up with the class.

I'll give it back, she told herself.

Just . . . maybe not

right away.

4

A BELLYFUL OF GLOOP

Trixie hung her coat in her cubby and sat down, but she couldn't focus on her work. Every time Spork glanced toward the cubbies, she wondered if he knew what she had done. Did Spork have X-ray vision? Could he see inside her coat?

She imagined the Gloop glowing brighter and brighter, until everyone could see it. She kept twisting in her seat to make sure it wasn't true.

"Trixie, do you need something from your cubby?" Mrs. Buckle asked.

Trixie turned back around.

When the bell rang for lunch, Trixie was first in line. She couldn't wait to get out of the classroom, away from the hidden Gloop.

Spork loved the cafeteria, even after Grace explained that he was supposed to *slide* his tray along the metal rails, not ride it. And when he saw the chicken nuggets, he squeaked happily, "Space fungus! Yum!"

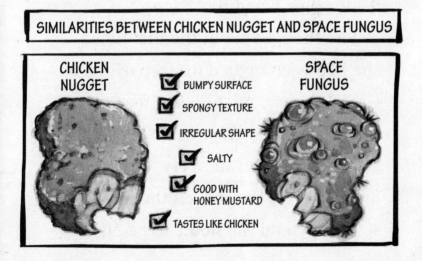

SIMILARITIES BETWEEN CHICKEN NUGGET AND SPACE FUNGUS

CHICKEN NUGGET

SPACE FUNGUS

☑ BUMPY SURFACE
☑ SPONGY TEXTURE
☑ IRREGULAR SHAPE
☑ SALTY
☑ GOOD WITH HONEY MUSTARD
☑ TASTES LIKE CHICKEN

Trixie and her friends led Spork to their usual table. Other children squeezed in, too, asking Spork a zillion questions.

"Is everybody on your planet orange?"

"How old do you have to be to get a flying saucer?"

"Are you homesick yet?"

Trixie picked at her lunch. She felt as if she had a bellyful of Gloop.

She thought about the first time she had been invited to sleep over at Grace's house. As soon as Grace's mom turned out the lights, Trixie felt so homesick she began to cry. Grace was disappointed, but she got the phone so Trixie could call home to be picked

up. She didn't hide the phone so Trixie
would be forced to stay.

But I didn't want to leave the PLANET,
Trixie told herself. *It's not the same!*

At afternoon recess, all the children
ran to play on the flying saucer again.
Trixie sat on the monkey bars alone.
She watched Spork, waiting for him
to realize his Gloop was gone. But he
didn't seem to think of it at all.

Back in the classroom, Trixie was
careful not to look toward her cubby.
She tried to push the Gloop out of her
mind.

Then Mrs. Buckle told the class it was
time to Drop Everything and Read just
as Spork was carrying a tub of markers
to the shelf.

"Okay!" Spork said and dropped the tub.

As the markers rolled across the floor, the children scrambled to help pick them up. Mrs. Buckle closed her eyes and shook her head.

"Did I do something wrong?" Spork asked Trixie. "I was just following directions." He pointed to the RESPECT poster. "I guess I still have a lot to learn about your Earthling rules!"

Trixie looked at the poster.

Had she been treating Spork with respect when she hid his Gloop? Was that how she would want to be treated? How would she like to be stuck on a strange alien planet with no way home?

Maybe Spork wasn't the only one who had a lot to learn about respect.

Trixie made up her mind. She ran to her cubby, then back to Spork.

"I took your Gloop." Her eyes stung as she pushed it toward him. "I'm sorry."

The startled alien reached for the Gloop just as Trixie let go. They watched it fall.

"Uh-oh," Spork squeaked.

5

GLOOP FIXES EVERYTHING

BOOM!

A light flashed. Blinking, Trixie found herself sitting on the floor. She looked around. The classroom looked . . . changed, somehow.

"Hey!" one of the boys exclaimed. "My shirt got tucked in! And my shoes are tied!"

An instant later, everyone was yelling.

"Look at the reading corner! The books are all in ABC order!"

"How did my cubby get so neat?"

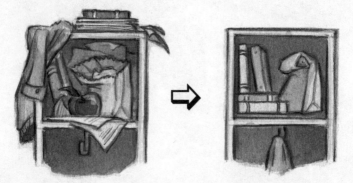

"My old pencil grew a new eraser!"

"These jeans had a hole in the knee.
Where did it go?"

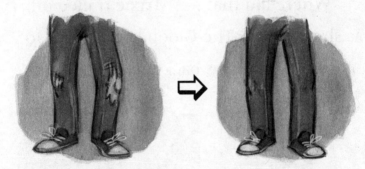

"Look at my math worksheet! I got
half the answers wrong, and now they're
right!"

Trixie stood up.

"What happened?" she asked Spork.

"I told you," the alien said. "Gloop fixes everything."

"But . . . why were you so worried?" Trixie asked. "Isn't that good?"

Spork pointed. "Jo Jo doesn't think so."

The hamster crouched in a corner of the cage, glaring at a large chunk of wood.

"Where did that . . ." Trixie trailed off as she realized. The Gloop had "fixed" Jo Jo's wood shavings back into wood!

"That's not so bad," Trixie said.

"Yeah, but you never know what Gloop will fix if you're not careful," Spork said. "One time I dropped Gloop in an asteroid belt and—well, I almost got kicked out of the Galaxy Scouts."

The mention of the Galaxy Scouts reminded Trixie of what she had done.

She hung her head. "Now that your Gloop exploded all over the classroom, there isn't any left to fix your flying saucer. And it's all my fault."

"Oh, don't worry about that!" Spork said. "I've got more Gloop."

"You . . . you do?" she asked.

The alien nodded. "I use a ton of it. My troop leader says Gloop was made for me." Spork paused. "I wonder what he means by that?"

Trixie's mind whirled. So Spork wasn't stuck on Earth after all!

She was relieved . . . but also sad. She looked up at the clock. Any second now, the bell would ring for the end of the day and Spork would have to go.

Trixie sniffled. "Goodbye, Spork. I hope you get your Solo Explorer badge."

"Goodbye?" he asked. "Are you leaving?"

"No, you are!" Trixie said. "Didn't you say you only had one day?"

Spork looked puzzled. Then he brightened.

"Ohhhhhhh . . . you thought I meant one EARTH day. But your days are so short! One Earth day isn't nearly long enough to learn your customs and earn my Solo Explorer badge."

"You mean . . . on your planet, the days are longer?" Trixie asked.

Spork nodded. "Much longer. One of our days is the same as a few weeks on Earth." He frowned. "Or was it months? Or years? I knew I should have paid better attention in Milky Way Math!"

Trixie looked around the room. Mrs. Buckle had most of the children calmed down, although Jack was still complaining, "But I *liked* my backpack with the zipper broken!"

It had been the weirdest, most exciting, most *different* day ever in third grade, Trixie thought happily. And best of all, tomorrow might be even weirder.

Spork was here to stay!

BEEP BEEP BEEP.

Huh, the light on my transmitter isn't going on. I must have bonked it when I crashed. Good thing I've got plenty of Gloop to fix it with! I've got a lot to tell my troop.

Of course, I probably don't need to tell them EVERYTHING. I mean, those crayons LOOKED delicious. Anybody would make that mistake.

And I won't say anything about the mess I made when I dropped all those markers, because that wasn't even my fault. How was I supposed to know the teacher didn't really mean "drop everything"?

Hey, wait, when did the light go on?

Um . . . if you guys heard all that . . . I was just kidding.

Really.

Ha ha.

Ha.

Greetings!

So far the Galaxy Scouts haven't signed up any young Earthlings. But I'll bet they will! Here's some stuff to get you ready for when the time comes— and it's all right out of the Scout training manual!

—Spork

Planet of Perils

Once I had to check out a planet named Grup. It should have been named Trouble! You'll see what I mean—just take a look at the picture and fill in the blanks below with the peril that best completes the sentence.

1. I was stung by a _____.
2. I got tangled in a _____.
3. I was squeezed by a _____.
4. I was spiked by a _____.
5. I was chased by a _____.
6. I fell into a _____.

THE PERIL BANK

Bristly Boa   Horrid Hornet   Stinky Swamp

Bad-Tempered Bush   Dagger-Toothed Hound

Vicious Vine

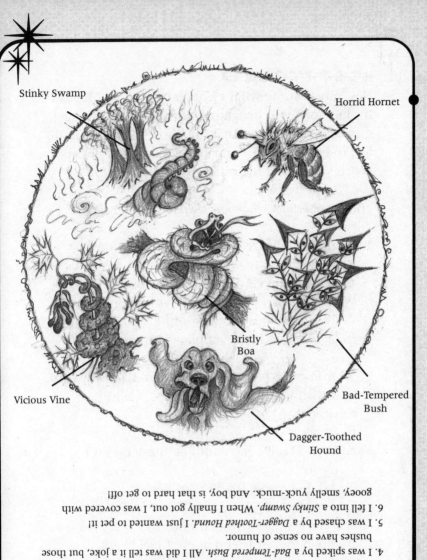

Stinky Swamp

Horrid Hornet

Bristly Boa

Vicious Vine

Bad-Tempered Bush

Dagger-Toothed Hound

Answers: Maybe you're wondering why all this bad stuff happened to me, but keep reading and you'll see. I really couldn't help it!

1. I was stung by a *Horrid Hornet*. I kind of sat on it. Ouch!
2. I got tangled in a *Vicious Vine*. I was stuck for a long time—but then I remembered I had a Galaxy Snipper Clipper!
3. I was squeezed by a *Bristly Boa*. At first I thought it just liked me.
4. I was spiked by a *Bad-Tempered Bush*. All I did was tell it a joke, but those bushes have no sense of humor.
5. I was chased by a *Dagger-Toothed Hound*. I just wanted to pet it!
6. I fell into a *Stinky Swamp*. When I finally got out, I was covered with gooey, smelly yuck-muck. And boy, is that hard to get off!

R-E-S-P-E-C-T the E.T.

Hey, guys! Know what I just learned about? Respect! It's kind of about imagining how it feels to be the other person and treating them just the way you'd like to be treated. So I made up this quiz. I bet you get the hang of it in no time!

(There can be more than one right answer.)

1. Your friend is tired and wants to go home. You say:
   a. "Think you could stay a little longer?"
   b. "If you stay, you can play with my pet flarg."
   c. "We can have yummy borple if you stay!"
   d. "Leave and I'll never play with you again!"

2. Your friend has a new Zab Blaster. It's really cool. You wish you had one, so you:
   a. Grab it.
   b. Break it.
   c. Say, "I really like your Zab Blaster. Can I try it?"
   d. Ask to borrow it and then keep it.

3. You have a date with a friend. You want to play Pagbo, but your friend doesn't feel like it.
   a. You say, "Then I'm going to play with somebody else!"
   b. You turn around and go home.

c. You say, "Okay. I don't mind playing something else now, but can we play Pagbo the next time we get together?"

d. You say, "Okay, what do you want to do?"

4. You're visiting a friend and you're thirsty.
   a. You say, "Where's the pluppleberry juice?"
   b. You say, "Can I please have some juice?"
   c. You start looking around for some juice.
   d. You say, "I want juice, and I want it NOW."

Answers: The best way to answer these questions is to imagine that you are your friend. Then think how you'd feel in the same spot!

1. *a.* That shows respect because you're not trying to keep your friend from doing what he wants to do—plus you're letting him know you had a good time with him! Two other answers are okay, too—*b* and *c.* It's fine to think of ways to make staying longer more fun for your friend. But if your friend still wants to leave, give up and let him!

2. *c.* This is an easy one. Would you like your friend to grab or keep your Zab Blaster? NO.

3. *c* and *d.* These are both good answers because you're giving your friend a chance to choose. (I like *c* because I *really* like to play Pagbo!)

4. *b.* The other choices would make it hard for your friend to say no. Maybe he's saving his pluppleberry juice. I like to save mine for space missions!

Space Facts: True or False

Every Galaxy Scout who will be traveling near Earth has to take this True or False test. See how you do!

1. A star lasts forever.
2. Twelve Earthlings have walked on the moon.
3. The creatures who live on Earth's moon are called Moonlings.
4. Most of the Earth is covered with water. Watch where you land!
5. The sun travels around the Earth.
6. Zibo is the planet closest to the sun.
7. Earth scientists have seen more than a trillion stars in the universe.
8. There are more chickens than people on Earth (but more people than chickens in space).

Answers:

1. False. Stars are born—and they die, too.
2. True. And all twelve Earthlings were U.S. astronauts.
3. False. There's no such thing as a Moonling! And nothing lives on the moon!
4. True. About 70% of Earth is covered by water. It's wet and splashy. Earthlings move around on it in things they call boats.
5. False. The Earth travels around the sun.
6. False. There is no planet Zibo. I made it up! The planet nearest the sun is Mercury.
7. True. Earthlings have a thing they call a telescope that lets them see far, far away. So far they have seen more than a trillion stars in the universe. In fact, they've seen a *septillion* stars—that's 1,000,000,000,000,000,000,000,000.
8. True. There are lots and lots of chickens on Earth—they are very popular. But so far, not a single chicken has made it into space.

MEET THE AUTHOR AND ILLUSTRATOR

NAN WALKER is the alias of a children's author whose books can be found at many Earthling training centers. She plans to earn her first Galaxy Scouts badge by adding chocolate syrup to the Milky Way. What could possibly go wrong?

JESSICA WARRICK has illustrated lots of picture books about dogs, cats, and kids, but she is mostly interested in drawing aliens, for some strange reason. She does a pretty good job acting like an Earthling . . . most of the time.

Spork just landed on Earth, and look, he already has lots of fans!

"Young readers are going to love this series! Spork is a funny and unexpected main character. Kids will love his antics and sweet disposition. Teachers and parents will appreciate the subtle messages embedded in the stories. The kids in the stories genuinely like each other, which I found refreshing. I will be giving these books to my young friends."—**Ron Roy**, author of A to Z Mysteries, Calendar Mysteries, and Capital Mysteries

"I'm so glad Spork landed on Earth! His misadventures are playful and sweet, and I love the clever wordplay!" —**Becca Zerkin**, former children's book reviewer for the *New York Times Book Review* and *School Library Journal*; past member of the Bank Street College Children's Book Committee

"Kids will love reading about Spork. Parents, teachers, and librarians will love reading aloud this series to those same kids."—**Rob Reid**, author of *Silly Books to Read Aloud*

Don't miss these Spork adventures!

Respect

Honesty

Responsibility

Courage

Check out these other series from Kane Press

Animal Antics A to Z®
(Grades PreK–2 • Ages 3–8)
Winner of two *Learning* Magazine Teachers' Choice Awards
"A great product for any class learning about letters!"
—*Teachers' Choice Award reviewer comment*

Let's Read Together®
(Grades PreK–3 • Ages 4–8)
"Storylines are silly and inventive, and recall Dr. Seuss's *Cat in the Hat*
for the building of rhythm and rhyming words."—*School Library Journal*

Holidays & Heroes
(Grades 1–4 • Ages 6–10)
"Commemorates the influential figures behind important American
celebrations. This volume emphasizes the importance of lofty ambitions
and fortitude in the face of adversity…"—*Booklist* (for *Let's Celebrate Martin
Luther King Jr. Day*)

Math Matters®
(Grades K–3 • Ages 5–8)
Winner of a *Learning* Magazine Teachers' Choice Award
"These cheerfully illustrated titles offer primary-grade
children practice in math as well as reading."—*Booklist*

The Milo & Jazz Mysteries®
(Grades 2–5 • Ages 7–11)
"Gets it just right."—*Booklist*, starred review (for *The Case
of the Stinky Socks*); *Book Links'* Best New Books for the Classroom

Mouse Math®
(Grades PreK & up • Ages 4 & up)
"The Mouse Math series is a great way to integrate math and literacy into
your early childhood curriculum. My students thoroughly enjoyed these
books."—*Teaching Children Mathematics*

Science Solves It!®
(Grades K–3 • Ages 5–8)
"The Science Solves It! series is a wonderful tool for
the elementary teacher who wants to integrate reading
and science."—*National Science Teachers Association*

Social Studies Connects®
(Grades K–3 • Ages 5–8)
"This series is very strongly recommended…."—*Children's Bookwatch*
"Well done!"—*School Library Journal*

KANEPRESS.com